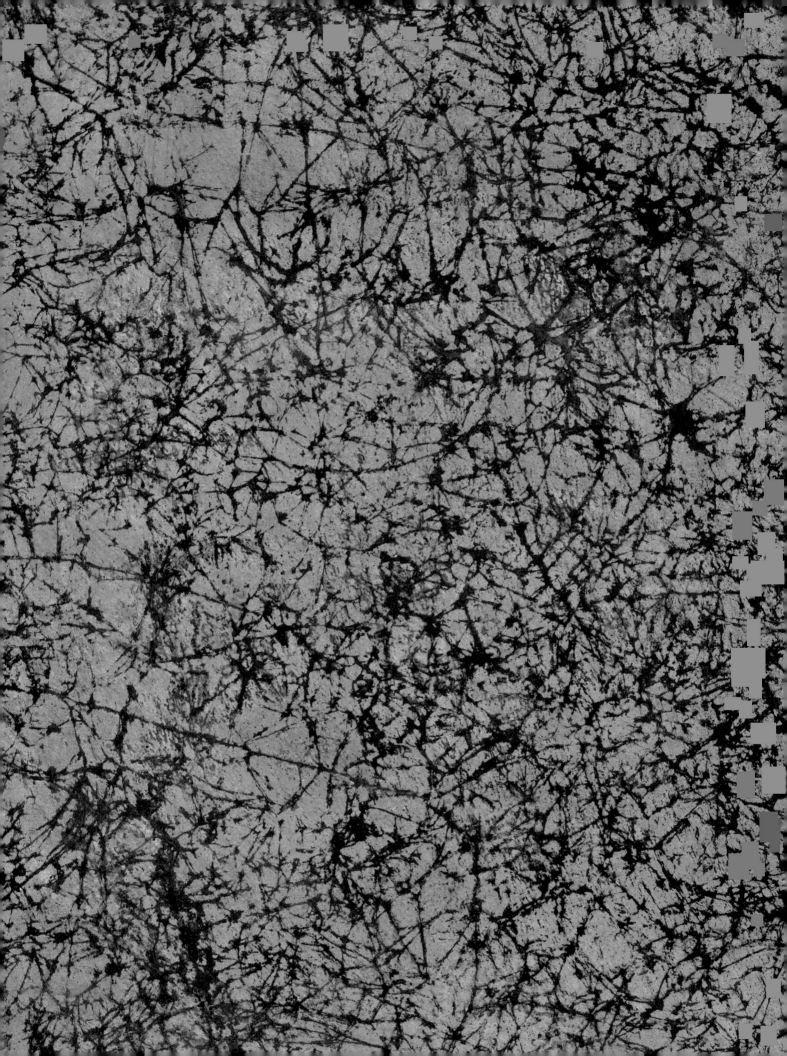

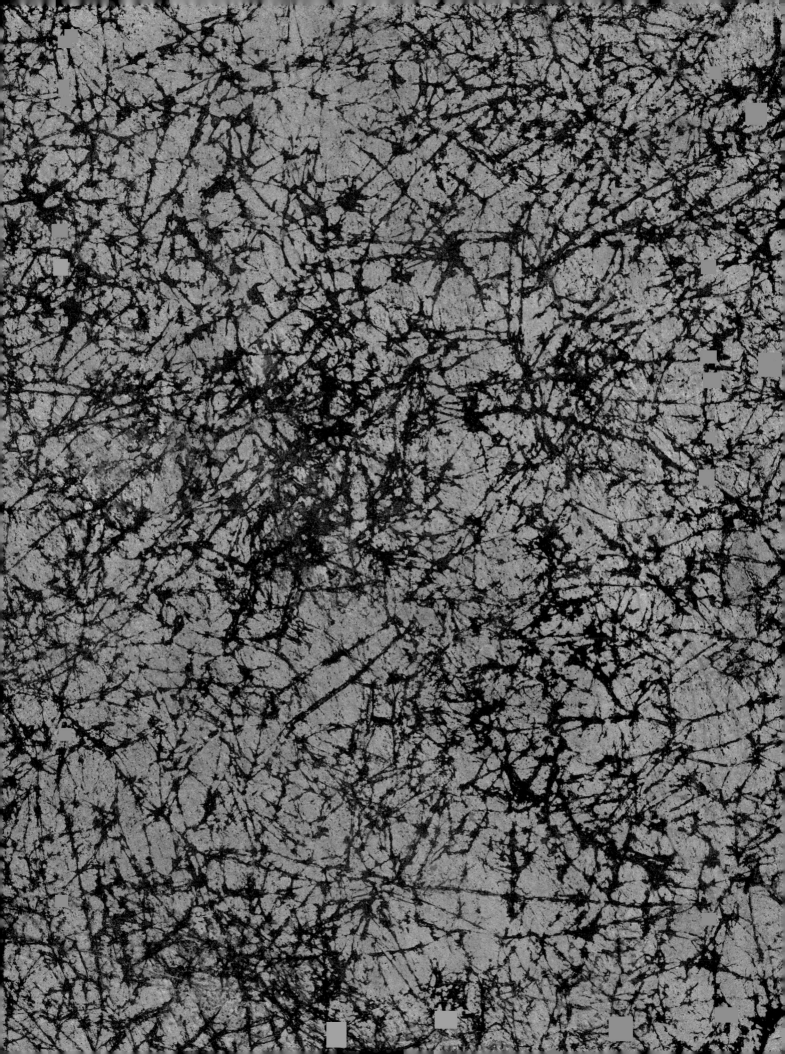

To the memory of Shraddhanand Swami. RT
For Matina and Joanna. KP

Text © Robin Tzannes 1993

Illustrations © Korky Paul 1993

Originally published in America by
Scholastic, Inc.

This paperback edition published by
Scholastic Inc., 730 Broadway, New York, NY 10003,
by arrangement with Oxford University Press

First Scholastic printing, December 1993

Printed in Hong Kong

SANJI
and the
BAKER

Written by Robin Tzannes
Illustrated by Korky Paul

Scholastic, Inc.

New York Toronto London Auckland Sydney

When Sanji was a young man,
he traveled a great deal.
He sailed across stormy seas.

FRATSIA

He traveled over hot, open deserts.

One day he arrived in the fabled city of Fratsia, a dazzling place where merchants traded in spices, gems, and colorful silks.

Sanji decided to stay there a while.

He found a room that suited him
perfectly. It was small and simple but
quite cozy.

Best of all, it was right above the Baker's shop.

In the morning Sanji awoke to
a delicious smell wafting up from
the bakery.

Dark, crusty bread hot from the oven.
Warm, sweet rolls filled with juicy currants.
Crunchy biscuits covered in sesame seeds.

Sanji stepped onto his balcony and took a
deep breath. He whiffed and sniffed the
heavenly aroma. Mmm . . . fresh cinnamon buns.
He just had to have one.

In the bakery Sanji bought the tiniest cinnamon bun in the shop.

'I've been on my balcony enjoying the wonderful smells from your oven,' he told the Baker.

'Oh, you have, have you?' growled the Baker. He narrowed his eyes and glared at Sanji.

That evening when Sanji came home, he stood on his balcony to inhale the lovely smells that rose from the bakery.

Sweet coconut cakes and orange spice, date nut loaves and walnut whirls.

Sanji stood dreamily, sniffing
and whiffing. He didn't see the
Baker staring up at him.
This went on for many days.

Suddenly one evening the Baker banged angrily on Sanji's door. 'Thief!' he cried. 'You are stealing my smells!'

Sanji was astonished. 'What are you talking about?' he asked, opening the door.

'Don't think I haven't seen you, standing on your balcony whiffing and sniffing!' shouted the Baker.

'You smell my bread every morning. You smell my cakes every evening!'

'I *must* be paid for those smells!'

'Nonsense!' said Sanji. 'Those smells come up here by themselves! I haven't stolen anything from you!'

The Baker shook his fist at Sanji.

'So you refuse to pay! Then I'll take you to court. The Judge will see that I get my payment!'

So they went to court.
The Baker told his story and
the Judge listened carefully.
Then he questioned Sanji.
　'Do you enjoy those smells?'
　'Yes, your Honor,' Sanji replied.
　'And have you ever paid for them?'
　'No, your Honor, I haven't.'
　The Judge thought for a long time.
　At last he said, 'Both of you will
return to court tomorrow morning
at nine o'clock. Sanji, you will
bring five silver coins.'

Sanji was miserable.
He didn't have five silver coins.

He would have to borrow them
from his friends.
And how would he ever
pay them back?

The next morning at nine o'clock the Judge entered the court room. Sanji stood quietly, with his head bowed.

The Baker was there too, grinning and rubbing his greedy hands together.

The Judge spoke first to Sanji.

'Have you brought the silver coins?'

'Yes, your Honor,' he answered in a whisper.

The Judge took a large copper
bowl and placed it before him.
He told Sanji to throw the coins,
one at a time, into the bowl.

To the Baker he said,
'Now listen carefully . . .'

CLINK
TINKLE
CLATTER
CLANG
RATTLE

The first coin clinked
into the bowl.

The second coin tinkled
beside it.

The third coin clattered.

The fourth coin clanged.

The fifth coin rattled
onto the pile.

The Judge turned to the Baker.
'Did you hear those coins clatter
and clink?'
'Yes, your Honor,' replied the Baker,
looking hungrily at the bowl of coins.
'And did you enjoy the sound of their
rattle and clang?' asked the Judge.
'Oh, yes! I certainly did!'
cried the Baker.

'Good,' said the Judge. 'Because *that* was your payment.'

'And you, Sanji,' he continued, 'may have
your five silver coins back.'
'Thank you, your Honor.'

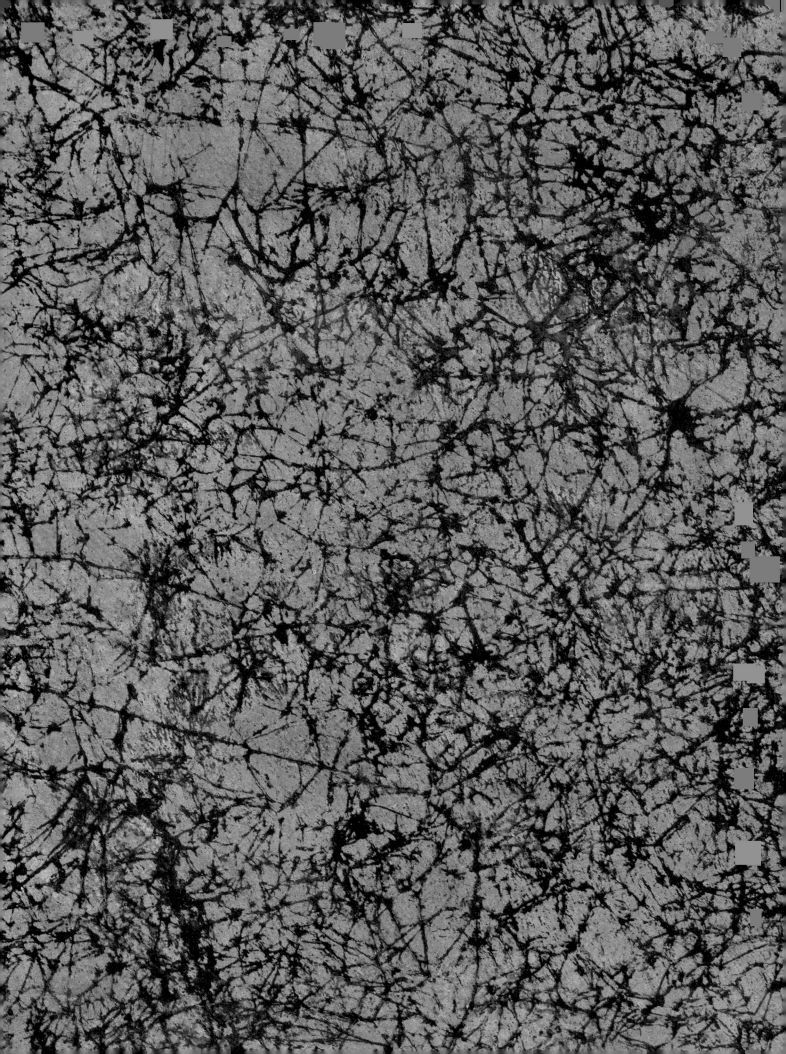

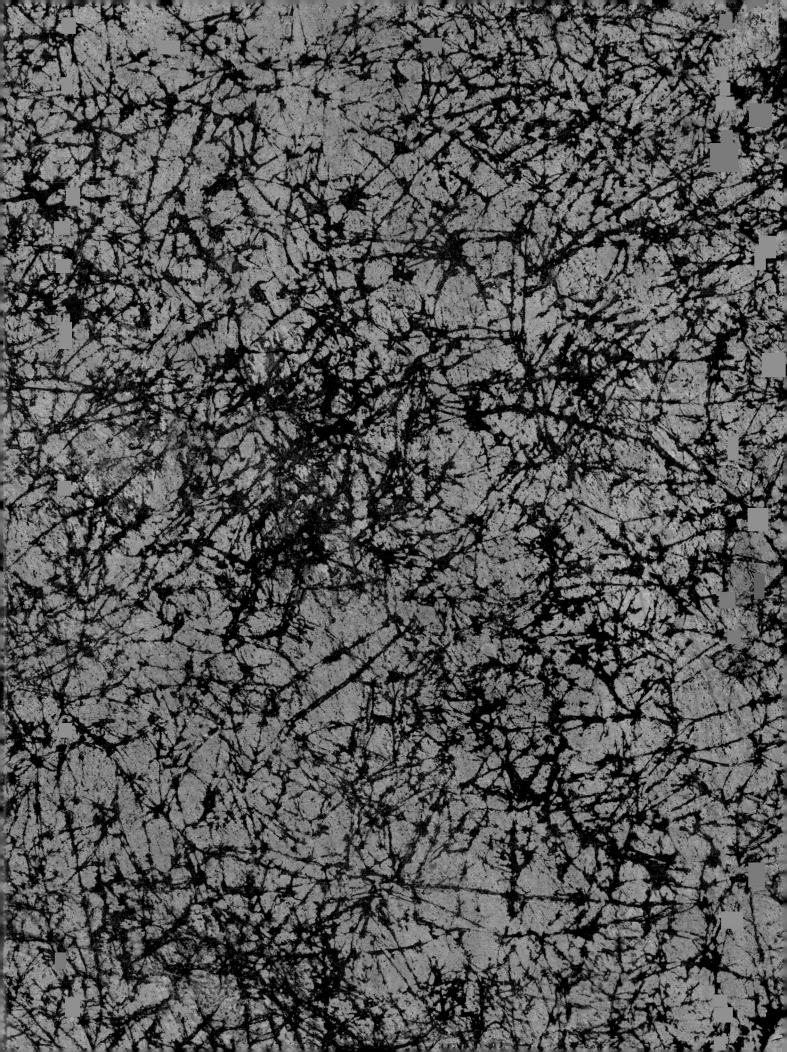